COOL CATS

Burmese

by Betsy Rathburn

Note to Librarians, Teachers, and Parents:

Blastoff! Readers are carefully developed by literacy experts and combine standards-based content with developmentally appropriate text.

Level 1 provides the most support through repetition of high-frequency words, light text, predictable sentence patterns, and strong visual support.

Level 2 offers early readers a bit more challenge through varied simple sentences, increased text load, and less repetition of high-frequency words.

Level 3 advances early-fluent readers toward fluency through increased text and concept load, less reliance on visuals, longer sentences, and more literary language.

Level 4 builds reading stamina by providing more text per page, increased use of punctuation, greater variation in sentence patterns, and increasingly challenging vocabulary.

Level 5 encourages children to move from "learning to read" to "reading to learn" by providing even more text, varied writing styles, and less familiar topics.

Whichever book is right for your reader, Blastoff! Readers are the perfect books to build confidence and encourage a love of reading that will last a lifetime!

This edition first published in 2017 by Bellwether Media, Inc.

No part of this publication may be reproduced in whole or in part without written permission of the publisher. For information regarding permission, write to Bellwether Media, Inc., Attention: Permissions Department, 5357 Penn Avenue South, Minneapolis, MN 55419.

Library of Congress Cataloging-in-Publication Data

Names: Rathburn, Betsy, author.
Title: Burmese / by Betsy Rathburn.
Other titles: Blastoff! Readers. 2, Cool Cats.
Description: Minneapolis, MN : Bellwether Media, Inc., 2017. | Series: Blastoff! Readers. Cool Cats | Audience: Ages 5-8. | Audience: K to grade 3. | Includes bibliographical references and index.
Identifiers: LCCN 2016032031 (print) | LCCN 2016042914 (ebook) | ISBN 9781626175617 (hardcover : alk. paper) | ISBN 9781681032825 (ebook)
Subjects: LCSH: Burmese cat–Juvenile literature.
Classification: LCC SF449.B8 R38 2017 (print) | LCC SF449.B8 (ebook) | DDC 636.8/24–dc23
LC record available at https://lccn.loc.gov/2016032031

Text copyright © 2017 by Bellwether Media, Inc. BLASTOFF! READERS and associated logos are trademarks and/or registered trademarks of Bellwether Media, Inc. SCHOLASTIC, CHILDREN'S PRESS, and associated logos are trademarks and/or registered trademarks of Scholastic Inc.

Editor: Christina Leaf   Designer: Lois Stanfield

Printed in the United States of America, North Mankato, MN.

Table of Contents

What Are Burmese?	4
History of Burmese	8
Heavy Like Bricks	12
Curious Cats	18
Glossary	22
To Learn More	23
Index	24

What Are Burmese?

Burmese cats are known for their beautiful, deeply colored **coats**.

People love to pet their short, **glossy** fur.

Burmese are **affectionate** cats. They love to cuddle under blankets.

These cats are **vocal**, too. They talk a lot!

History of Burmese

The Burmese **breed** began with a cat named Wong Mau. She came to the United States from Burma in 1930.

Dr. Joseph Thompson

Her owner was Dr. Joseph Thompson. He **bred** her with a Siamese cat.

Wong Mau's kittens were popular. People loved the sweet, new breed!

By the 1970s, Burmese were the third most popular cat breed in the United States. Today, they are still a favorite among cat lovers.

Heavy Like Bricks

Burmese are medium-sized cats. They have **sturdy** bodies. Some people say they are heavy like bricks!

Burmese Profile

wide, round eyes

round head

sturdy body

Weight: 8 to 12 pounds (4 to 5 kilograms)

Life Span: 16 to 18 years

They have round heads and short noses.

Wide, golden eyes make these cats stand out.

Burmese have **solid** coats. Sometimes their bellies have lighter fur.

Burmese Coats

Many Burmese cats are **sable**. Other colors include blue, **champagne**, and **platinum**.

Curious Cats

Burmese are **curious** cats. They explore every part of the house.

They also like to learn tricks. Some Burmese will show off skills to earn treats.

These cats love to be near people. They will follow their owners from room to room.

Burmese get along with other cats, too. Some will even play with dogs!

Glossary

affectionate—loving

bred—purposely mated two cats to make kittens with certain qualities

breed—a type of cat

champagne—light yellowish brown

coats—the hair or fur covering some animals

curious—interested or excited to learn or know about something

glossy—shiny

platinum—light gray

sable—dark brown

solid—one color

sturdy—strongly built

vocal—expressing sound often or loudly

To Learn More

AT THE LIBRARY

Felix, Rebecca. *Siamese*. Minneapolis, Minn.: Bellwether Media, 2016.

Murray, Julie. *Burmese Cats*. Edina, Minn.: Abdo Pub., 2003.

Sexton, Colleen. *The Life Cycle of a Cat*. Minneapolis, Minn.: Bellwether Media, 2011.

ON THE WEB

Learning more about Burmese cats is as easy as 1, 2, 3.

1. Go to www.factsurfer.com.

2. Enter "Burmese cats" into the search box.

3. Click the "Surf" button and you will see a list of related web sites.

With factsurfer.com, finding more information is just a click away.

Index

affectionate, 6
bellies, 16
blankets, 6
bodies, 12, 13
bred, 9
breed, 8, 10, 11
Burma, 8
coats, 4, 16, 17
colors, 17
cuddle, 6
curious, 18
explore, 18
eyes, 13, 15
follow, 20
fur, 5, 16
heads, 13, 14
kittens, 10
learn, 19
life span, 13
noses, 14
owners, 20

play, 21
Siamese, 9
size, 12, 13
skills, 19
talk, 7
Thompson, Joseph, 9
treats, 19
tricks, 19
United States, 8, 11
vocal, 7
Wong Mau, 8, 10

The images in this book are reproduced through the courtesy of: petographer/ Alamy, front cover; Zuzana Tillerová, pp. 4-5 (subject); Costi Iosif, pp. 4-5 (background); Jagodka, pp. 5, 14, 17 (inset upper right and inset upper left), 19; Eden Breitz/ Alamy, pp. 6, 21; S_Photo, p. 7 (background); FotoJagodka/ Deposit Photos, p. 7 (subject); Geoffrey Kuchera/ Deposit Photos, p. 8; jojosmb, p. 9; www.blackandtansiamese.com, p. 9 (small); Lifeontheside, p. 10; Alinute Silzeviciute, p. 11; Steppenwolf/ Alamy, pp. 12-13; mdmmikle, p. 13; Zuzule, pp. 14-15 (subjects); BLUR LIFE 1975, pp. 14-15 (background); Juniors Bildarchiv GmbH/ Alamy, pp. 16-17; otsphoto, p. 17 (inset lower left); Linn Currie, p. 17 (inset lower right); Tierfotoagentur/ Alamy, pp. 18-19; Juniors/ Juniors/ SuperStock, p. 20.